AMELIA BEDELIA'S MASTERPIECE

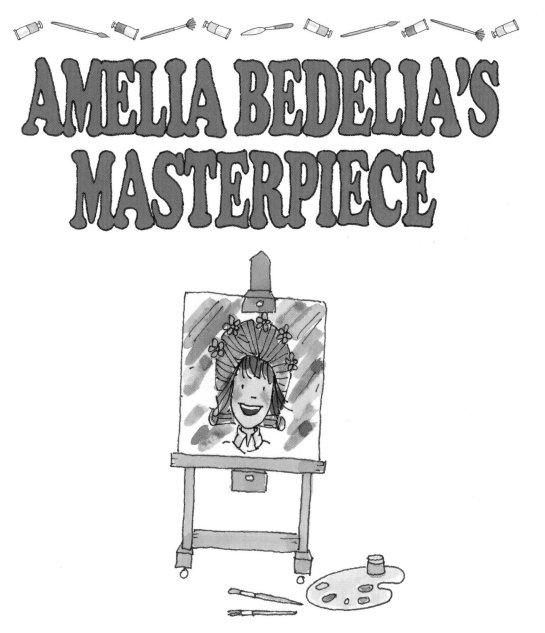

BY HERMAN PARISH

PICTURES BY LYNN SWEAT

Greenwillow Books, *An Imprint of* HarperCollins*Publishers*

Amelia Bedelia's Masterpiece

Text copyright © 2007 by Herman S. Parish III

Illustrations copyright © 2007 by Lynn Sweat

All rights reserved. Manufactured in China.

www.harpercollinschildrens.com

Watercolor and black pen were used to prepare the full-color art.

The text type is Times.

Library of Congress Cataloging-in-Publication Data

Parish, Herman.

Amelia Bedelia's masterpiece / by Herman Parish ; pictures by Lynn Sweat.

p. cm.

"Greenwillow Books."

Summary: Amelia Bedelia visits an art museum,

where her confusion leads to surprising results.

ISBN-13: 978-0-06-084355-7 (trade bdg.) ISBN-10: 0-06-084355-1 (trade bdg.)

ISBN-13: 978-0-06-084356-4 (lib. bdg.) ISBN-10: 0-06-084356-X (lib. bdg.)

[1. Art museums—Fiction. 2. Museums—Fiction. 3. Humorous

stories.]   I. Sweat, Lynn, ill. II. Title.

PZ7.P2185Arm 2007 [E]— dc22 2006020010

First Edition 10 9 8 7 6 5 4 3 2 1

Greenwillow Books

For my pal Jay Jasper
—H. P.

To Elynor
—L. S.

The minute Amelia Bedelia

walked into the art museum,

she knew it would be an exciting day.

"Wow," said Amelia Bedelia.

"Look at all of this amazing art.

The people look interesting, too."

One person stood out from the others.

Everyone was staring at him.

"It is not polite to stare,"

said Amelia Bedelia.

"I will make him feel at home."

She walked over to the man and said,

"Excuse me. What are you looking at?"

He did not answer, so she said,

"It must be very interesting."

He didn't say a word, so she said,

"May I borrow your binoculars?"

He did not move a muscle.

"I will get his attention," said Amelia Bedelia.

She reached out to tap him on the shoulder.

Suddenly, a voice behind her boomed out.

"Do not touch the art!"

"Yipes!" said Amelia Bedelia.

She jumped behind the man and hid.

"Mrs. Rogers!" said Amelia Bedelia.

"You scared the daylights out of me."

"I am so sorry," said Mrs. Rogers.

"You are not allowed to touch the art."

"Is his name Art?" said Amelia Bedelia.

"No, he . . . it . . . is art," said Mrs. Rogers.

"It is a sculpture called *Birdwatcher.*"

"The artist fooled me," said Amelia Bedelia.

"It's tough to tell the people from the art."

"Come along," said Mrs. Rogers.

"Let me show you some other works of art."

  They walked across the main gallery.

"Thanks for coming," said Mrs. Rogers.

"The museum needs your help today."

"My pleasure," said Amelia Bedelia.

"It's fun to be surrounded by art."

"This isn't the art," said Mrs. Rogers.

"This is the museum gift shop."

"This is a store?" said Amelia Bedelia.

"You mean this stuff is for sale?"

"Oh my, yes," said Mrs. Rogers.

"These are genuine reproductions."

"I get it," said Amelia Bedelia.

"These are real fakes."

"I guess so," said Mrs. Rogers.

"That is one way to put it."

Amelia Bedelia saw a familiar face

staring at her from a shelf.

"Look here," said Amelia Bedelia.

"Who does this remind you of?"

"It's Cousin Alcolu!"

said Mrs. Rogers.

"Were his ancestors Roman?"

"They sure were," said Amelia Bedelia.

"His family was roaming all over

the United States."

"I see," said Mrs. Rogers, with a laugh.

"Let's buy it for his birthday."

"How much is it?" said Amelia Bedelia.

"It is a bargain," said Mrs. Rogers.

"The real thing would be priceless."

"Price less?" said Amelia Bedelia.

"Without a price, it would be free."

"Not really," said Mrs. Rogers.

"Compared to the original art,

this reproduction is worthless."

"Worth less?" said Amelia Bedelia.

"Worth less than what?"

"Than the real thing," said Mrs. Rogers.

"That sounds wacky," said Amelia Bedelia.

"If the real thing doesn't have a price,

how could it be worth more?"

Just then, a man walked up to them.

"Amelia Bedelia," said Mrs. Rogers,

"meet the director of the museum."

"Pleased to meet you," the director said.

"My name is Arthur Stiles,

but you can call me Art."

"Nice to meet you," said Amelia Bedelia.

"You have been very busy, Art.

This museum is full of works of Art."

Art laughed and said,

"I wish I were that talented.

I take care of the art collection.

I can't take credit for it."

"I'm a collector, too,"

said Amelia Bedelia.

"Of what?" said Art.

"Paintings? Sculptures?"

"Aluminum foil," said Amelia Bedelia.

She reached in her purse

and pulled out a big shiny ball of foil.

"She's very handy," said Mrs. Rogers,

"and she's our newest volunteer."

"That is terrific," said Art.

"You could work here in the store."

"Great," said Amelia Bedelia.

"With my employee discount,

I will save Mrs. Rogers lots of money."

"Amelia Bedelia!" said Mrs. Rogers.

"Do not be so forward."

Amelia Bedelia took a step backward.

"If you think about discounts," said Art,

"you must have a head for figures."

"Really?" said Amelia Bedelia.

"I have an idea," said Art.

"Look around the museum.

See what interests you.

Then we can figure out

a way for you to help."

"Sounds like a plan," said Amelia Bedelia.

"Before I go,

may I buy this?"

"Certainly,"

said Art.

"I will even give you

my discount on that bust."

"Bust?" asked Amelia Bedelia.

"Is it a bargain because

it's busted?"

"It isn't broken," said Mrs. Rogers.

"Of course not," said Art.

"A 'bust' is a sculpture of the head,

shoulders, and chest."

"I see," said Amelia Bedelia.

"You can see the real thing," said Art,

"if you walk through that door."

Amelia Bedelia said thanks and good-bye.

Then she took the shopping bag

and headed off to explore.

Amelia Bedelia found the real bust right away.

"Oh my gosh," said Amelia Bedelia.

"Here is Cousin Alcolu, just like Art said.

And there is no price on it,

just like Mrs. Rogers said."

Amelia Bedelia took the bust

out of her bag.

She unwrapped it and compared it

to the one on the pedestal.

"The bust we bought is in better shape.

I know how to help the museum.

I will loan the museum our bust

while I take the price less one home

and clean it up."

Amelia Bedelia swapped the busts.

She carefully wrapped

the museum bust,

put it in her bag, and tidied up.

AH-CHOO!

"Ah-CHOO!" Amelia Bedelia sneezed.

"Ancient art is so musty and dusty.

Maybe I should try something newer."

Amelia Bedelia saw a sign.

She did exactly what it said.

"I see why they called this one

Banana Split. It sure is!"

"Ouch!

This reminds me of the day

Mr. Rogers ran his car

into the garage door."

"Did they hang this one upside down?

I'll bet the floor was covered with paint.

Looks like somebody already cleaned it up."

When Amelia Bedelia turned the corner,

she was shocked by what she saw.

"My goodness," said Amelia Bedelia.

"Art would be mad to see this mess

in his museum.

I'll straighten it up right now."

FAMILY ROOM

Amelia Bedelia got the cleaning cart

from the other gallery and went to work.

"How strange," said Amelia Bedelia.

"All of the food is plastic.

No wonder they left it behind."

Amelia Bedelia worked as fast as she could.

She finished up

just as Art walked into the gallery.

"Here you are," said Art.

"What have you been up to?"

"See for yourself," said Amelia Bedelia.

Art couldn't believe his eyes.

"Amelia Bedelia!" shouted Art.

"What have you done?"

"I cleaned up," said Amelia Bedelia.

"I am a housekeeper.

I know exactly what I'm doing."

"It wasn't a mess," said Art.

"This was a work of art."

"Please," said Amelia Bedelia.

"Don't blame yourself, Art.

This was the work of a slob."

"No, it wasn't," said Art.

"A famous modern artist

installed this work of art.

She called it *Family Room*."

"Whose family?" said Amelia Bedelia.

"Did a family of raccoons live here?"

"We disagree about art," said Art.

"But if you keep helping like this,

we won't have a museum left.

Do not touch one more thing! Please!"

Art walked away, shaking his head.

Amelia Bedelia felt terrible.

A teacher with students passed by

on a tour of the museum.

Amelia Bedelia decided to follow them.

In the next gallery, the students

gathered around their teacher.

"What type of painting is this?"

asked the teacher.

"It's a landscape,"

said a boy.

"And what kind of painting is this?"

she asked.

"That's a seascape," said a girl.

"And what is this?" the teacher asked.

Amelia Bedelia raised her hand.

"I know," she said. "It's a fire escape."

All the children laughed and giggled.

One of the students said, "It's a cityscape."

"That figures," said Amelia Bedelia.

"Are you Amelia Bedelia?"

asked the teacher.

"That's me," said Amelia Bedelia.

"I thought so," said the teacher.

"You helped at our school play last year."

"That was fun," said Amelia Bedelia.

"May I ask a favor?" said the teacher.

"One of my students doesn't feel well.

Would you please sit with him

until we complete our tour?"

"I'd be glad to," said Amelia Bedelia.

A boy with a sketchpad came forward.

"He is the best artist in our school,"

said the teacher. "His name is Drew."

"You'll fit right in," said Amelia Bedelia.

"The head of the museum is named Art."

The class moved on.

Drew began to draw.

"How do you feel?" asked Amelia Bedelia.

"Much better," said Drew.

"I was sick of hearing about art.

I want to *do* art."

"What do you like to draw best?"

asked Amelia Bedelia.

"I like figures," said Drew.

"Me, too," said Amelia Bedelia.

"My favorite is the number eight."

"Not number figures," said Drew.

"Human figures. People tell me

I have an eye for figures."

"That's funny," said Amelia Bedelia.

"I was told I have a head for figures."

"Well," said Drew. "Let's go figure."

They laughed and walked next door.

"Shhhh," said Drew. "A real artist."

"He must work for the museum,"

whispered Amelia Bedelia,

"making genuine reproductions."

"Maybe not," said Drew.

"Many artists copy famous paintings

to improve their skills."

They watched him paint some more.

"He is very talented," said Drew.

"He sure is," said Amelia Bedelia.

"I can't tell his copy from the real thing."

Another kind of painter walked by.

"Golly," said Amelia Bedelia.

"This place is full of painters."

They followed him into an empty gallery.

"Where are the paintings?"

asked Drew.

"You just missed them,"

said the painter.

"I repaint the walls

after an exhibit is over."

"Hey, I have an idea,"

said Amelia Bedelia.

"If you're going to

paint over these walls,

could Drew draw on them now, for fun?"

"Sure," said the painter. "Why not?

He can borrow my paints and brushes.

I won't need them until after lunch."

The painter sat down to eat a sandwich.

"Try my brush," said Amelia Bedelia.

"I'll go see if that other painter

has finished his masterpiece."

"See you later," said Drew.

"Look at that," said Amelia Bedelia.

"He replaced that old painting with his new one.

I'll bet he wants to take it home to clean it up."

The painter took the painting away.

"Good," said Amelia Bedelia.

"I can look without bothering him."

When she leaned forward,

some paint got on her bonnet.

"Uh-oh," said Amelia Bedelia.

"This paint is still wet."

Amelia Bedelia had a good idea.

She took out her ball of foil.

She used some foil

to cover the wet parts.

"That's better,"

said Amelia Bedelia.

"Folks won't get paint on themselves."

She went back to check on Drew.

Incredible figures covered the walls.

"Drew," said Amelia Bedelia.

"Way to go! This looks great."

"Thanks a lot," said Drew.

"I've never had so much fun!"

"Wow," said the painter.

"That kid is painting up a storm."

"No," said Amelia Bedelia.

"He paints figures, not weather."

Amelia Bedelia asked the painter,

"May I borrow your Wet Paint sign?

A painting next door is wet."

"That's impossible," said the painter.

"Those paintings have been dry

for years."

"Sure," said Amelia Bedelia.

"The original art is dry,

but the genuine

reproduction is wet."

"What? Show me!"

said the painter.

Along the way, they met a security guard.

Amelia Bedelia told him what she had seen.

The guard called the director on his radio.

"Think back, lady," said the guard.

"Did you see any sketchy characters?"

"Just one man," said Amelia Bedelia.

"He wasn't sketching,

he was painting."

Art ran into the gallery.

"Amelia Bedelia," said Art.

"*Now* what have you done?"

WET
PAINT

"I did you a favor," said Amelia Bedelia.

"Now people won't get

wet paint on themselves."

Art tore off the foil

and touched the painting.

"Don't touch!" said Amelia Bedelia.

"Mrs. Rogers will yell at you."

Art saw wet paint on his finger.

"A forgery!" he shouted.

"We've been robbed—sound the alarm!"

A report came over the radio.

"Painting has been found.

Suspect surrounded.

All guards to Roman gallery."

BONG·BONG!

BONG·BONG!

Everyone ran to the Roman gallery.

"Stand back!"

screamed the thief.

"Or I will smash this to bits!"

"Do what he says," said Art.

"That bust is priceless."

"No, it isn't," said Amelia Bedelia.

"Go ahead and break it if you like."

"Catch!" said the thief.

He tossed the bust into the air.

As everyone tried to grab it,

the thief made his getaway.

CRASH!

The guards raced after the thief.

"Close all the doors," ordered Art.

"He can't escape."

Art picked up the pieces of the bust.

"Amelia Bedelia!

Why did you tell him that?

This bust was priceless."

"Nope," said Amelia Bedelia.

"Here is the one without a price."

She pulled the bust out of her bag.

"The real bust!" said Art.

"You swiped it and saved it."

"I didn't swipe it," said Amelia Bedelia.

"I swapped it."

A guard ran up holding the disguise.

"I guess he got away," he said.

"Keep searching," said Art,

"and keep me posted.

Thank you, Amelia Bedelia.

You saved a priceless work of art

and foiled a forgery.

How can we ever repay you?"

"For starters,"

said Amelia Bedelia,

"how about a new bust

for Cousin Alcolu?"

"Done!" said Art.

"Anything else?"

"Follow me," Amelia Bedelia said.

"My head for figures tells me

that you will like

what you see."

She led Art to Drew.

Art was stunned.

"Did you draw this?"

he asked the painter.

"Not me," said the painter.

"That kid, Drew."

"What is his name?" said Art.

"That's it," said Amelia Bedelia.

"You are Art. He is Drew."

"Did someone call me?" asked Drew.

"I did, young man," said Art.

"I am the director of this museum.

Did you draw on my walls?"

"Yes, I did," said Drew.

"The painter said it would be okay."

"I don't call this okay," said Art.

"I call it fabulous!"

"You do?" said Drew.

"Absolutely," said Art.

"These figures are spectacular.

Your drawings will be our next show."

Drew hugged Amelia Bedelia.

"Drew," she said, "you are a true artist."

When Drew's class heard the news,

they all clapped and cheered.

"How exciting," said the teacher.

"This calls for another field trip

to see what Drew has drawn."

Amelia Bedelia walked back

to the museum entrance

to meet Mrs. Rogers

and head for home.

The museum was almost empty.

"For goodness' sake," said Amelia Bedelia.

"That artist has made another sculpture.

I'll brush off the fuzz stuck on its nose."

She took out her duster and . . .

AHH.
CHOO!

"You are not an art work,"

said Amelia Bedelia.

"You must be the art thief!"

The man dropped to his knees.

"Please don't turn me in," he said.

"Shame on you," said Amelia Bedelia.

"You have talent and so much to give.

How could you think about taking?"

The thief's eyes filled with tears.

"You are right," said the thief.

"I am sorry. I won't steal ever again."

"Promise?" she asked.

"I promise," he said.

"I believe you," said Amelia Bedelia.

"And I believe in you. Now good-bye."

He thanked her and vanished.

A moment later, Mrs. Rogers showed up.

"Who was that man?" she asked.

"Just some guy," said Amelia Bedelia.

"He likes to stand around in art museums."

"You see?" said Mrs. Rogers.

"You meet the most interesting people here.

Did you hear about the attempted robbery?"

They had a lot to talk about on the way home.

The next month, the art museum

opened the exhibit of Drew's work.

Cousin Alcolu's birthday

was on the very same day.

"Congratulations, Drew," said Mrs. Rogers.

"The whole town is proud of you."

"Thank you so much," said Drew.

"The show is a big hit," said Mr. Rogers.

"Thank Amelia Bedelia," said Art.

"Here you are," said Amelia Bedelia.

As Cousin Alcolu served cake, he said,

"Every year, Amelia Bedelia bakes

a coconut cake for my birthday."

"Mmmm," said Art to Amelia Bedelia.

"This piece of cake is *your* masterpiece."

"Thank you," said Amelia Bedelia.

"Speaking of masterpieces,

here is your birthday present."

As Cousin Alcolu took it,

the gift slipped out of the bag.

KEE-RASH!

"Oops!" said Cousin Alcolu.

"Not again," said Art.

"That was a bust," said Mrs. Rogers.

"It is now," said Mr. Rogers.

"It is in a million pieces."

"Don't worry," said Art.

"I know where to find another one."

"Thank you," said Amelia Bedelia.

"Just make sure it has a price."

"You can count on me," said Art.

"By the way, this came for you."

Amelia Bedelia unwrapped the package.

"This looks fantastic!" said Art.

"You've discovered another modern artist."

"Wow," said Drew. "Who did it?"

"There is a note," said Art.

Amelia Bedelia read it to herself.

"Turn around," said a man.

"I want to take your picture."

"No!" said Amelia Bedelia.

"You can't have it."

"Relax," said Art.

"He's a photographer."